Amazing APPLES

Consie Powell

Albert Whitman & Company
Morton Grove, Illinois

Absolutely the **P**erfect fruit to **P**ut in your **L**unchbox and **E**at later.

Out among the apple trees,
Robins sing,
Crickets chirp, and
Hungry spiders
Are building webs. Everything's
Ready for warm
Days of spring.

Lovely pale greens of
Early spring cover
All the budding trees.
Velvety blossoms will decorate
Every branch
Soon.

Buzzing
Excitedly, dusted with pollen,
Eager winged workers
Sip the sweet nectar.

Summer rays shine
Upon tiny apples that
Need warmth and light to grow.

Roots, leaves,
And branches drink
In splashing drops.
Now we're soaked, too!

Cut an apple

Open crossways, and your

Reward is an

Elegant little flower.

Who is this, peeking
Out from where I just bit?
Relax, he won't eat
Much.

Bring the baskets
Under these trees.
Soon they will
Hold more than
Enough fruit to
Last through winter.

Place each ripe apple
In the basket
Carefully. They
Keep better handled gently.

Vigorous trees of
All sizes and shapes yield
Rainbows of autumn fruit:
Ida Red, Jonathan, Arkansas Black,
Early Joe, McIntosh, Granny Smith, Buff,
Tobias, Delicious,
Ingram, Wolf River,
Esopus Spitzenburg, Rhode Island Greening,
Stayman, Rome, Prairie Spy, Lady, and more!

Can we fit a few more apples
In the press?
Drop them in, and crank with
Energy. Now watch the juice
Run into the bucket.

Delicate slices of
Ripe fruit shrivel
Into an
Easy and
Delicious snack.

Some
Apples taste best cut
Up, then cooked down to a
Chunky warm treat. Don't forget the
Extra cinnamon!

Pastry outside, apples **I**nside—who's ready to **E**at dessert?

Below the stairs
Are rows of
Shelves holding
Eleven pints of
Mother's apple butter,
Eighteen jars of jelly, and
Nine bushels of
Tree-ripened fruit.

White sparkles of
Ice cloak
Naked branches.
These generous trees have
Earned their
Rest.

About Apples

Look at the apples you eat for lunch.
Their ancestors, wild apples that grew
in southwestern Asia, were eaten by people
long ago. Ancient Romans and Greeks learned
to cultivate apples, and by a thousand years ago,
apples were grown throughout Europe.

In North America, the only native apples were
crabapples. When European settlers came, they
brought apple seeds to plant. Trees grown from
these seeds produced apples for animal food, cooking,
drying, eating out of hand, and cider, the most common
drink of the time.

But most of those apples tasted pretty ordinary. That's
because the fruit produced by a tree grown from a seed
will not be the same as the apple that made the seed.
Apples are a lot like people—each tree is different from the
parent trees that produced it.

Once in a while, however, a tree grown from a seed produces
a wonderful new *variety* (kind of apple). That's how American
favorites like McIntosh, Golden Delicious, and Northern Spy first
grew. To produce more of those special trees, or other trees with
desirable qualities, apple growers *grafted* buds from favorite trees
onto other apple trees to produce more of that variety of apple.

Almost all apple trees grown today are produced by grafting.
To graft a tree, a branch or bud of one tree is pressed into the cut
trunk or branch of another tree. The two plants grow together,
become one tree, and produce apples just like the tree from which
the branch or bud came. If buds of different varieties are grafted
to various branches of one tree, that single tree can produce
different varieties on different branches!

What Can You Do with Apples?

Have a Tasting Party: At the grocery store or farmers' market, get one of each variety of apple they sell. Cut thin slices of each apple and put them on a plate with name labels. Now taste and compare. If you nibble a cracker between each sample, you can taste the difference more easily.

What are the differences in color, texture, and taste? Have you found a new favorite?

Name an Apple: Apples are named for a place, a person, or perhaps a special trait. How do you think your favorite apples got their names? Can you guess how unusual varieties like Early Joe, Dumpling, Green Cheese, Little Benny, and Sheepnose got their names? What would you name an apple?

Dry Apples: Peel and core an apple or two, then cut in slices about ¼ inch thick. Run a string or thin dowel through the slices and hang them in a warm, dry place. In a couple of days the slices will be shriveled and dry to the touch. They are ready when they no longer feel cool and are just a bit springy when squeezed.

Bake an Apple: For a yummy treat, core a whole apple and put it in a shallow pan. Fill the core cavity with a little brown sugar, cinnamon, and raisins. Bake the apple at 350 degrees until it is soft and bubbly. To cook your apple in the microwave, put it on a microwave-safe dish. Cover with plastic wrap, turning back one corner. Bake for 4-6 minutes on the high setting.

This celebration of apples was created with

Help, inspiration, and support from

Annie, Rick, Bailey, Dylan,

Nokomis, Chess, Honey, Ebony,

Kim, Ken, Michael, Suzanne, Patricia, and the most

Special one of all, Rog.

Library of Congress Cataloging-in-Publication Data

Powell, Consie.
Amazing Apples / written and illustrated by Consie Powell.
p.   cm.
Summary: Simple poems in acrostic form describe an apple orchard
through the seasons, as well as the activities of the family that tends
the orchard. Includes a page of notes about apples.
ISBN 0-8075-0399-1
1. Apples—Juvenile poetry. 2. Apple growers—Juvenile poetry.
3. Children's poetry, American. [1. Apples—Poetry.
2. Apple growers—Poetry. 3. American poetry.] I. Title.
PS3566.O82655A83 2003
811'.54—dc21   2003002096

Text and illustrations copyright © 2003 by Constance Buffington Powell.
Published in 2003 by Albert Whitman & Company, 6340 Oakton Street,
Morton Grove, Illinois 60053-2723. Published simultaneously in Canada
by Fitzhenry & Whiteside, Markham, Ontario. All rights reserved. No part
of this book may be reproduced or transmitted in any form or by any
means, electronic or mechanical, including photocopying, recording,
or by any information storage and retrieval system, without permission
in writing from the publisher.
Printed in the United States of America.
10 9 8 7 6 5 4 3 2 1

The illustrations are created with hand-colored woodblock prints.
The design is by Consie Powell and Susan B. Cohn.

For more information about Albert Whitman & Company,
please visit our web site at www.albertwhitman.com.